THE TALE OF
PIGLING BLAND

THE TALE OF
PIGLING BLAND

BY

BEATRIX POTTER

Author of
" The Tale of Peter Rabbit," etc.

BLOOMSBURY BOOKS
in association with
FREDERICK WARNE

The reproductions in this book have been made using the most modern electronic scanning methods from entirely new transparencies of Beatrix Potter's original watercolours. They enable Beatrix Potter's skill as an artist to be appreciated as never before, not even during her own lifetime.

BLOOMSBURY BOOKS IN ASSOCIATION WITH FREDERICK WARNE

Published by the Penguin Group
Penguin Books Ltd, 27 Wrights Lane, London W8 5TZ, England
Penguin Books USA Inc., 375 Hudson Street, New York, N.Y. 10014, USA
Penguin Books Australia Ltd, Ringwood, Victoria, Australia
Penguin Books Canada Ltd, 10 Alcorn Avenue, Toronto, Ontario, Canada M4V 3B2
Penguin Books (N.Z.) Ltd, 182-190 Wairau Road, Auckland 10, New Zealand

Penguin Books Ltd, Registered Offices: Harmondsworth, Middlesex, England

Bloomsbury Books, an imprint of the Godfrey Cave Group,
42 Bloomsbury Street, London WC1B 3QJ

First published 1913 by Frederick Warne
This edition with new reproductions of Beatrix Potter's book
illustrations first published 1994

ISBN 185471 2195

Printed and bound in Great Britain by
William Clowes Limited, Beccles and London

THE TALE OF PIGLING BLAND

ONCE upon a time there was an old pig called Aunt Pettitoes. She had eight of a family: four little girl pigs, called Cross-patch, Suck-suck, Yock-yock and Spot;

and four little boy pigs, called
Alexander, Pigling Bland, Chin-
chin and Stumpy. Stumpy had
had an accident to his tail.

The eight little pigs had very fine
appetites. "Yus, yus, yus! they
eat and indeed they *do* eat!"

said Aunt Pettitoes, looking at her family with pride. Suddenly there were fearful squeals ; Alexander had squeezed inside the hoops of the pig trough and stuck.

Aunt Pettitoes and I dragged him out by the hind legs.

Chin-chin was already in disgrace; it was washing day, and he had eaten a piece of soap. And presently in a basket of clean clothes, we found another dirty little pig. "Tchut, tut, tut! whichever is this?" grunted Aunt Pettitoes.

Now all the pig family are pink, or pink with black spots, but this pig child was smutty black all over; when it had been popped into a tub, it proved to be Yock-yock.

I went into the garden; there I
found Cross-patch and Suck-suck
rooting up carrots. I whipped them
myself and led them out by the ears.
Cross-patch tried to bite me.

16

"Aunt Pettitoes, Aunt Pettitoes! you are a worthy person, but your family is not well brought up. Every one of them has been in mischief except Spot and Pigling Bland."

"Yus, yus!" sighed Aunt Pettitoes. "And they drink bucketfuls of milk; I shall have to get another cow! Good little Spot shall stay at home to do the housework; but the others must go. Four little boy pigs and four little girl pigs are too many altogether." "Yus, yus, yus," said Aunt Pettitoes, " there will be more to eat without them."

17

So Chin-chin and Suck-suck went away in a wheel-barrow, and Stumpy, Yock-yock and Cross-patch rode away in a cart.

And the other two little boy pigs, Pigling Bland and Alexander, went to market. We brushed their coats,

we curled their tails and washed
their little faces, and wished them
good-bye in the yard.

Aunt Pettitoes wiped her eyes
with a large pocket handkerchief,
then she wiped Pigling Bland's nose
and shed tears; then she wiped
Alexander's nose and shed tears;
then she passed the handkerchief
to Spot. Aunt Pettitoes sighed
and grunted, and addressed those
little pigs as follows:

"Now Pigling Bland, son Pigling Bland, you must go to market.
Take your brother Alexander by the
hand. Mind your Sunday clothes,
and remember to blow your nose"—

(Aunt Pettitoes passed round the handkerchief again)—" beware of traps, hen roosts, bacon and eggs; always walk upon your hind legs." Pigling Bland, who was a sedate little pig, looked solemnly at his mother, a tear trickled down his cheek.

Aunt Pettitoes turned to the other—" Now son Alexander take the hand "—" Wee, wee, wee! " giggled Alexander—"take the hand of your brother Pigling Bland, you must go to market. Mind—" "Wee, wee, wee!" interrupted Alexander again. " You put me out," said Aunt Pettitoes—

20

21

"Observe sign-posts and milestones; do not gobble herring bones—" "And remember," said I impressively, " if you once cross the county boundary you cannot come back.

Alexander, you are not attending. Here are two licences permitting two pigs to go to market in Lancashire. Attend, Alexander. I have had no end of trouble in getting these papers from the policeman."

23

Pigling Bland listened gravely; Alexander was hopelessly volatile.

I pinned the papers, for safety, inside their waistcoat pockets;

Aunt Pettitoes gave to each a
little bundle, and eight conversation
peppermints with appropriate
moral sentiments in screws of
paper.   Then they started.

26

Pigling Bland and Alexander
trotted along steadily for a mile;
at least Pigling Bland did. Alexander made the road half as long
again by skipping from side to side.
He danced about and pinched his
brother, singing—

" This pig went to market, this pig
stayed at home,
" This pig had a bit of meat—

let's see what they have given *us*
for dinner, Pigling ? "

Pigling Bland and Alexander
sat down and untied their bundles.
Alexander gobbled up his dinner
in no time; he had already eaten
all his own peppermints. " Give
me one of yours, please, Pigling . "

" But I wish to preserve them for emergencies," said Pigling Bland doubtfully. Alexander went into squeals of laughter. Then he pricked Pigling with the pin that had fastened his pig paper ; and when Pigling slapped him he dropped the pin, and tried to take Pigling's pin, and the papers got mixed up. Pigling Bland reproved Alexander.

But presently they made it up again, and trotted away together, singing—

" Tom, Tom, the piper's son, stole a pig
    and away he ran !

" But all the tune that he could play,
    was ' Over the hills and far away ! ' "

28

"What's that, young sirs? Stole a pig? Where are your licences?" said the policeman. They had nearly run against him round a corner. Pigling Bland pulled out his paper; Alexander, after fumbling, handed over something scrumply—

"To 2½ oz. conversation sweeties at three farthings "—" What's this? This ain't a licence." Alexander's nose lengthened visibly, he had lost it. " I had one, indeed I had, Mr. Policeman!"

" It's not likely they let you start without. I am passing the farm. You may walk with me." " Can I come back too?" inquired Pigling Bland. "I see no reason, young sir; your paper is all right." Pigling Bland did not like going on alone, and it was beginning to rain. But it is unwise to argue with the police; he gave his brother a peppermint, and watched him out of sight.

To conclude the adventures of
Alexander—the policeman saun-
tered up to the house about tea
time, followed by a damp subdued
little pig.   I disposed of Alexander
in the neighbourhood; he did fairly
well when he had settled down.

Pigling Bland went on alone dejectedly; he came to cross-roads and a sign-post—"To Market Town, 5 miles," "Over the Hills, 4 miles," "To Pettitoes Farm, 3 miles."

Pigling Bland was shocked, there was little hope of sleeping in Market Town, and to-morrow was the hiring fair; it was deplorable to think how much time had been wasted by the frivolity of Alexander.

He glanced wistfully along the road towards the hills, and then set off walking obediently the other way, buttoning up his coat against the rain. He had never wanted to go; and the idea of standing all

by himself in a crowded market, to be stared at, pushed, and hired by some big strange farmer was very disagreeable—

"I wish I could have a little garden and grow potatoes," said Pigling Bland.

He put his cold hand in his pocket and felt his paper, he put his other hand in his other pocket and felt another paper—Alexander's! Pigling squealed; then ran back frantically, hoping to overtake Alexander and the policeman.

36

He took a wrong turn—several wrong turns, and was quite lost.

It grew dark, the wind whistled, the trees creaked and groaned.

Pigling Bland became frightened and cried " Wee, wee, wee ! I can't find my way home !"

After an hour's wandering he got out of the wood ; the moon shone through the clouds, and Pigling Bland saw a country that was new to him.

The road crossed a moor ; below was a wide valley with a river twinkling in the moonlight, and beyond, in misty distance, lay the hills.

He saw a small wooden hut, made his way to it, and crept in-side—"I am afraid it *is* a hen house, but what can I do?" said Pigling Bland, wet and cold and quite tired out.

" Bacon and eggs, bacon and eggs!" clucked a hen on a perch.

"Trap, trap, trap! cackle, cackle, cackle!" scolded the disturbed cockerel. "To market, to market! jiggetty jig!" clucked a broody white hen roosting next to him. Pigling Bland, much alarmed, determined to leave at daybreak. In the meantime, he and the hens fell asleep.

In less than an hour they were all awakened. The owner, Mr. Peter Thomas Piperson, came with a lantern and a hamper to catch six fowls to take to market in the morning.

He grabbed the white hen roosting next to the cock; then his eye fell upon Pigling Bland, squeezed up in a corner. He made a singular remark—" Hallo, here's another !"—seized Pigling by the scruff of the neck, and dropped him into the hamper. Then he dropped in five more dirty, kicking, cackling hens upon the top of Pigling Bland.

The hamper containing six fowls and a young pig was no light weight; it was taken down hill, unsteadily, with jerks. Pigling, although nearly scratched to pieces, contrived to hide the papers and peppermints inside his clothes.

At last the hamper was bumped
down upon a kitchen floor, the lid
was opened, and Pigling was lifted
out.   He looked up, blinking, and
saw an offensively ugly elderly
man, grinning from ear to ear.

"This one's come of himself, whatever," said Mr. Piperson, turning Pigling's pockets inside out. He pushed the hamper into a corner, threw a sack over it to keep the hens quiet, put a pot on the fire, and unlaced his boots.

Pigling Bland drew forward a coppy stool, and sat on the edge of it, shyly warming his hands. Mr. Piperson pulled off a boot and threw it against the wainscot at the further end of the kitchen. There was a smothered noise— "Shut up!" said Mr. Piperson. Pigling Bland warmed his hands, and eyed him.

Mr. Piperson pulled off the other boot and flung it after the first, there was again a curious noise— " Be quiet, will ye ? " said Mr. Piperson. Pigling Bland sat on the very edge of the coppy stool.

44

Mr. Piperson fetched meal from a chest and made porridge. It seemed to Pigling that something at the further end of the kitchen was taking a suppressed interest in the cooking, but he was too hungry to be troubled by noises.

Mr. Piperson poured out three platefuls: for himself, for Pigling, and a third—after glaring at Pigling —he put away with much scuffling, and locked up.   Pigling Bland ate his supper discreetly.

After supper Mr. Piperson consulted an almanac, and felt Pigling's ribs; it was too late in the season for curing bacon, and he grudged his meal.   Besides, the hens had seen this pig.

He looked at the small remains of a flitch, and then looked undecidedly at Pigling.   "You may sleep on the rug," said Mr. Peter Thomas Piperson.

47

Pigling Bland slept like a top. In the morning Mr. Piperson made more porridge; the weather was warmer. He looked to see how much meal was left in the chest, and seemed dissatisfied—"You'll likely be moving on again?" said he to Pigling Bland.

Before Pigling could reply, a neighbour, who was giving Mr. Piperson and the hens a lift, whistled from the gate. Mr. Piperson hurried out with the hamper, enjoining Pigling to shut the door behind him and not meddle with nought; or "I'll come back and skin ye!" said Mr. Piperson.

It crossed Pigling's mind that if *he* had asked for a lift, too, he might still have been in time for market.

But he distrusted Peter Thomas.

After finishing breakfast at his leisure, Pigling had a look round the cottage; everything was locked up. He found some potato peelings in a bucket in the back kitchen. Pigling ate the peel, and washed up the porridge plates in the bucket. He sang while he worked—

" Tom with his pipe made such a noise,
He called up all the girls and boys—
" And they all ran to hear him play
" ' Over the hills and far away ! ' "

Suddenly a little smothered voice chimed in—

" Over the hills and a great way off,
The wind shall blow my top knot off!"

Pigling Bland put down a plate which he was wiping, and listened.

50

51

After a long pause, Pigling went on tip-toe and peeped round the door into the front kitchen. There was nobody there.

After another pause, Pigling approached the door of the locked cupboard, and snuffed at the key-hole. It was quite quiet.

After another long pause, Pigling pushed a peppermint under the door. It was sucked in immediately.

In the course of the day Pigling pushed in all the remaining six peppermints.

When Mr. Piperson returned, he found Pigling sitting before the fire; he had brushed up the hearth and put on the pot to boil; the meal was not get-at-able.

Mr. Piperson was very affable; he slapped Pigling on the back, made lots of porridge and forgot to lock the meal chest. He did lock the cupboard door; but without properly shutting it. He went to bed early, and told Pigling upon no account to disturb him next day before twelve o'clock.

Pigling Bland sat by the fire, eating his supper.

All at once at his elbow, a little voice spoke—" My name is Pigwig. Make me more porridge, please ! " Pigling Bland jumped, and looked round.

56

A perfectly lovely little black Berkshire pig stood smiling beside him. She had twinkly little screwed up eyes, a double chin, and a short turned up nose.

She pointed at Pigling's plate; he hastily gave it to her, and fled to the meal chest. "How did you come here?" asked Pigling Bland.

"Stolen," replied Pig-wig, with her mouth full. Pigling helped himself to meal without scruple. "What for?" "Bacon, hams," replied Pig-wig cheerfully. "Why on earth don't you run away?" exclaimed the horrified Pigling.

" I shall after supper," said Pig-
wig decidedly.

Pigling Bland made more porridge and watched her shyly.

She finished a second plate, got
up, and looked about her, as though
she were going to start.

"You can't go in the dark," said Pigling Bland.

Pig-wig looked anxious.

"Do you know your way by daylight?"

"I know we can see this little white house from the hills across the river. Which way are *you* going, Mr. Pig?"

"To market—I have two pig papers. I might take you to the bridge; if you have no objection," said Pigling much confused and sitting on the edge of his coppy stool. Pig-wig's gratitude was such and she asked so many questions that it became embarrassing to Pigling Bland.

He was obliged to shut his eyes and pretend to sleep. She became quiet, and there was a smell of peppermint.

" I thought you had eaten them, " said Pigling, waking suddenly.

"Only the corners," replied Pig-wig, studying the sentiments with much interest by the firelight.

" I wish you wouldn't; he might smell them through the ceiling," said the alarmed Pigling.

Pig-wig put back the sticky peppermints into her pocket; "Sing something," she demanded.

"I am sorry . . . I have tooth-ache," said Pigling much dismayed.

"Then I will sing," replied Pig-wig.
"You will not mind if I say iddy
tidditty? I have forgotten some of
the words."

Pigling Bland made no objection;
he sat with his eyes half shut, and
watched her.

She wagged her head and rocked
about, clapping time and singing
in a sweet little grunty voice—

    " A funny old mother pig lived in a
        stye, and three little piggies had she ;

    " (Ti   idditty idditty) umph, umph,
        umph ! and the little pigs said, wee,
        wee ! "

She sang successfully through three or four verses, only at every verse her head nodded a little lower, and her little twinkly eyes closed up.

> " Those three little piggies grew peaky and lean, and lean they might very well be ;
> " For somehow they couldn't say umph, umph, umph ! and they wouldn't say wee, wee, wee !
> " For somehow they couldn't say—

Pig-wig's head bobbed lower and lower, until she rolled over, a little round ball, fast asleep on the hearth-rug.

Pigling Bland, on tip-toe, covered her up with an antimacassar.

He was afraid to go to sleep himself; for the rest of the night he
sat listening to the chirping of the
crickets and to the snores of Mr.
Piperson overhead.

66

Early in the morning, between dark and daylight, Pigling tied up his little bundle and woke up Pig-wig. She was excited and half-frightened. But it's dark! How can we find our way?"

" The cock has crowed ; we must start before the hens come out ; they might shout to Mr. Piperson."

Pig-wig sat down again, and commenced to cry.

"Come away Pig-wig; we can see when we get used to it. Come! I can hear them clucking!"

Pigling had never said shuh! to a hen in his life, being peaceable ; also he remembered the hamper.

He opened the house door quietly and shut it after them. There was no garden; the neighbourhood of Mr. Piperson's was all scratched up by fowls. They slipped away hand in hand across an untidy field to the road.

The sun rose while they were crossing the moor, a dazzle of light over the tops of the hills. The sunshine crept down the slopes into the peaceful green valleys, where little white cottages nestled in gardens and orchards.

"That's Westmorland," said Pig-wig. She dropped Pigling's hand and commenced to dance, singing—

"Tom, Tom, the piper's son, stole a pig and away he ran !
"But all the tune that he could play, was 'Over the hills and far away !'"

"Come, Pig-wig, we must get to the bridge before folks are stirring." "Why do you want to go to market, Pigling ?" inquired Pig-wig presently. "I don't want ; I want to grow potatoes." "Have a peppermint ?" said Pig-wig. Pigling Bland refused quite crossly. "Does your poor toothy hurt ?" inquired Pig-wig. Pigling Bland grunted.

70

71

Pig-wig ate the peppermint herself and followed the opposite side of the road. "Pig-wig! keep under the wall, there's a man ploughing." Pig-wig crossed over, they hurried down hill towards the county boundary.

Suddenly Pigling stopped; he heard wheels.

Slowly jogging up the road below them came a tradesman's cart. The reins flapped on the horse's back, the grocer was reading a newspaper.

"Take that peppermint out of your mouth, Pig-wig, we may have to run. Don't say one word. Leave it to me. And in sight of the bridge!" said poor Pigling, nearly crying. He began to walk frightfully lame, holding Pig-wig's arm.

The grocer, intent upon his newspaper, might have passed them, if his horse had not shied and snorted. He pulled the cart crossways, and held down his whip. "Hallo! Where are *you* going to ?"—Pigling Bland stared at him vacantly.

Are you deaf? Are you going to market?" Pigling nodded slowly.

"I thought as much. It was yesterday. Show me your licence?"

Pigling stared at the off hind shoe of the grocer's horse which had picked up a stone.

The grocer flicked his whip— "Papers? Pig licence?" Pigling fumbled in all his pockets, and handed up the papers. The grocer read them, but still seemed dissatisfied. "This here pig is a young lady; is her name Alexander?" Pig-wig opened her mouth and shut it again; Pigling coughed asthmatically.

The grocer ran his finger down the advertisement column of his newspaper—"Lost, stolen or strayed, 10s. reward." He looked suspiciously at Pig-wig. Then he stood up in the trap, and whistled for the ploughman.

" You wait here while I drive on and speak to him," said the grocer, gathering up the reins.   He knew that pigs are slippery ; but surely, such a *very* lame pig could never run !

"Not yet, Pig-wig, he will look back." The grocer did so; he saw the two pigs stock-still in the middle of the road. Then he looked over at his horse's heels; it was lame also; the stone took some time to knock out, after he got to the ploughman.

"Now, Pig-wig, NOW!" said Pigling Bland.

Never did any pigs run as these pigs ran! They raced and squealed and pelted down the long white hill towards the bridge. Little fat Pig-wig's petticoats fluttered, and her feet went pitter, patter, pitter, as she bounded and jumped.

81

They ran, and they ran, and they ran down the hill, and across a short cut on level green turf at the bottom, between pebble beds and rushes.

They came to the river, they came to the bridge—they crossed it hand in hand—

then over the hills and far away
she danced with Pigling Bland!

THE END